MOUNTAIN TOP MYSTERY

Gertrude Chandler Warner
Illustrations: David Cunningham

ALBERT WHITMAN & Company Chicago

ISBN 0-8075-5293-3

Published simultaneously in Canada by General Publishing, Limited, Toronto.

10

Printed in the U.S.A.

Contents

CHAPTER 1

Grandfather in the Lead

It was a fine warm day in early summer. The Aldens—Henry, Jessie, Violet, and Benny—and their grandfather were just eating lunch. They had come to dessert of apple pie and cheese.

Benny rested his head on his hand. After awhile he said, "Grandfather, do you remember a few summers ago we wanted to go mountain climbing?"

"Yes, I remember, my boy."

"Well, do you remember we got cheated out of it? Joe and Alice had to go abroad and we couldn't go alone."

Henry said, "Benny will never forget that. We went to see Aunt Jane at Mystery Ranch instead."

Benny said, "Well, I wondered where we were going that summer, *if* we had gone. What mountain were we going to climb?"

"Benny, does all this mean you want to go mountain climbing?" asked Mr. Alden. He couldn't help laughing.

"Yes, it does," said Benny. "Maybe not the same mountain."

"No, indeed, it won't be," said Mr. Alden. "That year I was going to take you up in the Rockies. No more of that. We'll have to choose Old Flat Top because I don't want Violet getting all tired out with a long climb. And I don't want me getting all tired out either. The rest of you are tough enough."

Grandfather looked up to see that every Alden was looking at him. The four shining faces answered him. There were four nods.

"You do have the strangest ideas, Benny," said Jessie. "What put that into your head?"

"Well," said Benny, "I've been reading about that place in school."

"About Flat Top?" asked Violet.

"Oh, you have, have you?" said Henry. "You chose Flat Top yourself?"

"Right," said Benny. "I don't want to climb too much myself. I get lame."

Mr. Alden said, "Well, my answer is yes. Old Flat Top is easy enough for all of us, and yet it is interesting all the way up. And we'll all be able to get a good rest on the smooth top."

"Just like airplanes landing on an airplane carrier," said Benny.

"That's exactly right, my boy," said Grandfather. "Only this flat top is twice as big as a carrier."

Benny finished his apple pie and put down his fork. "Then the only question is *when*. Let's go right away."

Everyone laughed. Benny and Grandfather were so much alike. When they wanted anything they wanted it right away.

"What do you mean by right away?" asked Grandfather, smiling. "You mean this minute? If you do, we could go this minute, very easily. It is only a day's trip. You climb up Flat Top, eat lunch, and climb down. There is just time in one day. Nobody spends the night there."

"How do you know all this, Grandfather?" asked Henry.

"Oh, I had a friend who made that trip last summer. He said it was exactly right for his wife, and they had a fine time. Near the foot of the mountain is a general store. The men give you poles and a lunch and directions. They always leave a lot of firewood all cut for a campfire to cook your lunch on the flat top. This place isn't for real mountain climbers. It's for old men and children."

Henry laughed. He knew that it was a real mountain. Grandfather was having a good time teasing them.

"Do you mean we can really go today?" asked Jessie.

"Well, no," Grandfather answered. "I should say tomorrow would be better because we must have a full day. We can drive to Old Flat Top in two hours. What time do you want to get up, Benny? You're the sleepy one."

"I'll get up at five," said Benny. "I did when we went to the lighthouse."

"So you did. Five it is. Lay out some sport clothes. Better take some extra clothes. We may want to go on somewhere else. And another thing, we can't take Watch. He'll just be in the way."

"That's right," said Henry. "He will do nothing but whine. He doesn't like to see us do anything dangerous."

Mr. Alden looked thoughtful and then said, "I believe that Dr. Percy Osgood is working somewhere in the range not too far from Old Flat Top. How about it, Benny, does that name mean something to you?"

Benny shook his head. But Henry said, "Osgood? It means something to me. He was the author of a book on geology I read for a college course last year."

"Right!" Grandfather said. "Percy is on a hunt for some fossils. If John Carter can find out where he is for me we might pay him a visit. I haven't seen Osgood for years, but I don't suppose he's changed much."

The Aldens went to pack and Grandfather made a phone call to John Carter. It was too bad Benny wasn't around to hear some of the plans being made. But he and the others were busy packing.

There was not much sleep in the Alden house that night. At five o'clock everyone was wide awake and downstairs eating breakfast.

"I have two flashlights," said Henry, "and some batteries and the binoculars. You can see the view better."

Grandfather said, "We'll get the lunch at the store and water and either coffee or cold drinks in bottles. We can buy anything we need."

The day was beautiful. It was warm even in the early morning. They all knew it would be cooler on Flat Top, and they each had a warm sweater.

When they reached the mountain range, Violet said, "Oh, isn't this lovely!"

"That's Old Flat Top," said Benny, pointing. It was the lowest mountain in the range. Other peaks went much higher into the sky. Some looked blue in the distance. Others looked violet. Others looked green. But Flat Top was so near it looked green almost all the way up. The top was all solid rock.

"Hey!" said Henry. "There is the store. It seems to be made of logs." He stopped the car at the door and they all went into the store. Old Flat Top towered right over them.

"Just right," said Benny. "Not too high. Not too steep. Just right, just a good healthy climb and a grand view at the top." Then he thought, "Isn't it queer that this store man seems to know Grandfather?"

The two men were shaking hands, and Grandfather just said, "Fit us out for Flat Top, won't you?"

The man said, "You each need a pack on your back to carry your lunch. You'll need five poles. I should think that would be enough. You'll find the path is well marked, but there's only one. And remember that there is no other path down."

"I'd like to go first," said Benny.

"I'm sorry to disagree with you, Benny," said Mr. Alden. "I should like to go first."

"Oh," said Benny, "of course, you should go first. That's OK."

"Thanks," said Mr. Alden.

Up they went. It was true that the path was well marked. The trees were marked with knotted strips of red cloth. It was a little hard in some places, but the poles were a great help. Each climber had a pack on his back.

Up and up they went. Violet was right behind Grandfather. Benny still wished he could be the leader, but he thought he had better mind his grandfather at this point.

It took the Aldens three hours to reach the first stop.

"See the sign?" said Henry. "Lunch Here. The man said we must eat just half of our lunch here."

"I have never been so hungry in my life," said Benny.

"Oh, yes, you have!" joked Henry. "Almost every

meal you eat. And be careful how much water you drink. That's the thing we have to save."

Soon they were ready to go on. When they were almost at the top they noticed there were no more bushes, no more trees, no more grass. It was all gray rock.

Grandfather looked ahead. He could see the last two steps very well. He noticed that the last step was a

big one, and he was glad he had gone first. With his pole, he reached the very top where it was flat. He turned around and gave a hand to Violet. Then he helped Jessie up, and reached way down to help Benny. With his pole, Henry climbed up by himself.

They all looked around. "This is as big as our own front yard," said Jessie.

"What a view," said Benny. "The town is over there, and nothing but woods there at the foot of the mountain."

Henry said, "Here is the woodpile for campfires and a fireplace. This is where we can cook the rest of our lunch."

It never entered anyone's head, even Grandfather's, that a fire might be needed to keep them warm.

CHAPTER 2

Hold On, Benny!

My, I'm glad we have sweaters," said Henry. "The wind blows harder up here." He pulled his brown sweater on over his head.

The others put on their sweaters and then they sat down in a row.

"What a view!" said Jessie. They looked out over the valley. They felt as if they were very high up.

Grandfather said, "Benny, you come over and sit by me. I want to talk to you. You know a boy ought to learn a thing the first time he is told. Of course he can learn it the second time and maybe the third time. But he will save a lot of time for himself by learning the first time. I am telling you not to go near the edge, and I shall say nothing more about it. Is that clear?"

Grandfather almost never spoke in that sort of voice.

"Oh, yes indeed!" cried Benny. "I learned that before you got through talking. I don't like the edge myself."

Henry looked around at Flat Top. There was a small hump in the middle. "Look at the wavy lines in the rocks," he said. "White and black and gray. Wouldn't a geologist find this interesting?"

Everyone looked around. Violet said, "It looks like the waves of the sea."

Grandfather said, "That is just what they look like, but they are waves of rock. Probably millions of years ago what we are standing on now was covered by the ocean."

Henry said, "This low mountain may once have been near the ocean floor. It was pushed up to where it is now."

Benny threw his head back and laughed. He said, "I'll bet the old dinosaurs paddled around here."

"Maybe dinosaurs were here when this was a swamp," said Jessie.

"I wish I had brought my camera," said Henry.

"Oh, I wish you had," said Violet.

Mr. Alden was looking at the great stretch of woods below. He said, "I don't think anyone has ever cut those trees. I'd hate to get lost there."

Benny looked at his wristwatch. "I hope someone besides me will say it's time to eat," he said.

Violet said, "I am willing to be the one." She patted Benny's shoulder.

Jessie said, "Let's sit here and plan what we will do."

"That's the housekeeper in you, Jess," said Henry. "If we are going to cook that hamburger we'll have to get a fire started. Let's find the wood."

Mr. Alden sat still and watched them.

"Well, there are certainly all kinds of wood," said Benny. "Big and little. And look, there is a kettle and a frying pan."

"That kettle is for hot water, I think," said Violet. "Just throw a little coffee in, and there will be Grandfather's coffee."

"Freshly made," said Grandfather.

"Those men at the store thought of everything," said Benny. "Here's the fireplace with a back rock to keep off the wind." He was beyond the little hump.

"Well, I guess we're all set," said Henry.

Everybody had a job. The two boys built the fire, for even Benny knew how to start a good fire. The girls made cakes of the hamburger and took out the bacon.

"I think we had better fry the bacon first," said Jessie, and the girls soon had the crisp slices lying on a paper napkin.

"Where shall we put the grease, Grandfather, when we get through?"

"Give it to me," said Mr. Alden, "and I will show you. Wait till I get all set."

Grandfather, without a smile, got down flat on his stomach and crawled slowly to the edge. "Now I'll take the pan," he said. Everyone tried not to laugh—Mr. Alden looked so funny. With a straight face, Mr. Alden took the pan and poured the hot fat down the rocky mountainside. He backed slowly until he was far from the edge. Then he said, "That grease went almost straight down for half a mile. That's why you can't go down or up except on our trail."

"Oh, you did look funny," said Benny. "I could hardly help laughing."

"Neither could I," said Mr. Alden. "Now we can laugh all we want."

Indeed when anyone thought of Grandfather pouring grease straight down the mountain, it was hard to stop laughing at all.

"Now the hamburger," said Henry. "Just about room for six in this pan."

Jessie passed him the hamburger cakes. They started at once to give out a delicious smell.

Soon Henry gave the orders, "Get a plate and a bun and a piece of cheese and a paper napkin, and be all ready for your hamburger."

"We'll get a bottle of Coke, too," said Benny.

"Right," said Henry. "And I will put Grandfather's black coffee in one of these cups."

Never did food taste better. They made it last a long time.

"I think this is the first time," said Jessie, "that we ever had anything left over from a picnic. I couldn't eat all my hamburger, and neither could Violet. We have five buns and one hamburger left."

"You will see that I didn't quite finish my big hamburger either," said Grandfather.

Benny's loud voice was heard saying, "Save it—save every crust and every crumb. I have a feeling I might use it later in the day."

The Alden family picked up all their papers and cups and burned them in the fire. Grandfather said, "Save my coffee, too. I have a feeling I might like it just before we go. We go at exactly four o'clock."

Violet shook every drop out of an empty Coke bottle. She filled the bottle with coffee.

Henry saw what she was doing. He said, "Just

dump the coffee grounds on the rocks. The wind will blow them away."

"When we go down," said Benny, "how about letting me go first?"

"All right," Grandfather agreed, "you lead the way."

They put the scraps of food in a paper bag and at exactly four o'clock Benny got ready to back down.

Benny said, "The first step will hold both my feet."

"So will the second one," said Henry.

Benny reached down carefully with one foot for the first step. He held onto the edge tightly. It was a long way down to the step and he almost wished he had let Grandfather or Henry go first.

"Let me take one of your hands," Henry said. "Take your time and you'll be all right."

Benny swung his other foot down but still kept Henry's hand. The next step was not quite so steep.

With one foot on the second step Benny was just about to let Henry go. Then with no warning it happened—one moment Benny's foot was on the step, the next he was reaching wildly for a foothold.

With a noise like thunder the stone step went crashing down the mountain side. As it rolled, it knocked loose stones and boulders in a regular mountain slide.

"Help!" Benny shouted, hanging on to Henry and trying to catch at anything that would not crumble and break loose.

Grandfather threw himself down and grabbed Benny by his free arm. Henry got a better grasp. Jessie took the back of his sweater and the three pulled Benny to the top and safety.

Benny lay perfectly still on his side, breathing hard. "Gramps," he said, "it will take me three days to get over this."

Benny had never called his grandfather "Gramps" before, and nobody had ever seen him quite so still. Mr. Alden knelt down to comfort him. He said, "Benny, you put your mind on this. Forget the step. Just think that your life was saved for something special and try to wonder what it is."

Benny sat up at once. "I *was* saved, wasn't I?" he cried. "Maybe I'll be a mountain climber. Or a scientist."

Jessie and Violet both looked pale. They knew what a narrow escape Benny had had. The noise of the rocks crashing down, Benny's shout, the rescue—it had all happened so quickly.

Henry looked around the rocky top of the mountain. He did not want to frighten the girls, but he knew that the only way down was gone. The rocky sides of Old Flat Top gave no spot to get a foothold.

Mr. Alden said, "Now let's plan what we'll do. We are safe here, but we'll be cold. We certainly can't get down now."

Henry said, "Won't the ranger and the man in the store notice when we don't come down?"

Mr. Alden gave Henry a look. Then he said, "There are a lot of things that they may do. One thing seems sure. We'll have to spend the night up here. This is the end of the summer and it will be dark soon."

Henry said, "Perhaps they heard those rocks coming down."

"Yes," said Violet. "They crashed like thunder."

"They probably did hear the noise," said Mr. Alden. "I don't think we need to worry, but perhaps we'd better build a fire. They will see it when it gets dark."

Henry had a feeling that Mr. Alden knew something that the children did not, but he went right to work and everyone helped to build a roaring fire.

Violet's teeth were chattering. She said, "The f-f-fire f-f-feels good. I didn't know I was so c-c-cold."

"That's because you nearly lost me, Violet," said Benny. "Haven't you ever heard of shivering from fright?"

It soon began to get quite dark. Still Grandfather did not seem to be worried. Suddenly they all heard a strange whirring noise.

"It sounds like an airplane," said Benny. "I'll bet it's a helicopter."

Henry cried, "That's Grandfather for you! I'll bet he planned that in case of trouble." Grandfather smiled.

It was indeed a helicopter. First it went high over the flat top, winked its lights, and then hovered over the family. The pilot had a megaphone.

He called down, "Are you all right?"

Five voices shouted, "Yes!"

"We can't take you off in the dark," the pilot called. "We'll have to wait until morning. But I am going to drop five sleeping bags. Keep your fire going, and we'll be around in the morning. Now all of you stand behind the hump."

The whole family did so. Down came five sleeping bags, one by one. The helicopter whirred away.

Jessie said, "I guess they didn't know that we are short on food. It's lucky we saved everything from lunch that we did not eat. I wonder if we should eat the leftovers for supper."

"Maybe we should save our food for the morning," Violet said. "We might have to wait for quite awhile."

"Good idea," agreed Grandfather. "As long as we are warm we can stand being a little hungry."

Benny added, "I guess I got being hungry scared right out of me—at least for now."

Grandfather said, "You know the old saying about an ill wind that blows no good."

"It wasn't a wind, it was a rock slide," Benny said.

Mr. Alden said, "We might as well get into these sleeping bags to keep warm."

When they were all in the sleeping bags they sat in a row.

Benny said, "We'd look funny if there were anyone to see us."

They all looked down over the dark country. Many lights of the town showed at the left, but not a light at the right.

In a little while Jessie said, "You know, I think I see a faint light in the woods. You don't suppose anyone is in trouble, do you?"

"I don't see it," said Mr. Alden. "Oh yes, I do, too. It's very faint, but it stays right in one place."

Benny asked, "How could anyone live in the woods? I wonder what the light is."

Mr. Alden was glad to have anything interesting to talk about because he knew the night would be long. "When we get down," he said, "we will find out what the light is. The rangers may know, and if they don't, we'll find out anyway."

The stars came out. They were very bright.

"I don't really mind going to bed tonight," said Benny. "I'm in bed."

Jessie whispered to Henry, "He seems to be all right."

"Thanks to Grandfather," whispered Henry. "He certainly said the right thing to Ben."

Mr. Alden and Henry decided to take turns putting wood on the fire during the night. There was plenty of wood. They all lay down in a row. Benny was on one side of Grandfather, and Violet was on the other.

Benny sounded sleepy as he said, "I'm coming over closer to you, Grandfather, if you don't mind."

"Come ahead, my boy," said Mr. Alden.

"You know, Grandfather," said Benny, "I must have been seeing things. When that big rock gave way, I thought I saw an enormous hole behind it."

"Maybe you really did see a hole," said Grandfather. "I have heard of holes in mountains."

But by this time, Benny was asleep.

CHAPTER 3

Waiting for Rescue

When Henry awoke he thought even before he opened his eyes, "The helicopter will come at sunrise." Then he opened his eyes and blinked.

The whole mountain top was covered with thick fog. Henry turned his head to look at Jessie. She was close enough to touch, but he could hardly see her.

Benny called, "I'm awake, Henry. Foggy, isn't it?"

Henry propped himself up on one elbow. "I wonder if it is often foggy like this in the morning. I guess when we're not up so high we don't pay any real attention."

Grandfather said, "The mountain top is always covered with fog in the early morning. That's why campers don't stay here overnight. But the fog will soon go away."

Henry said, "One thing is sure. We must stay close together every minute."

Everyone understood what Henry meant. It would be dangerous to move about too much and perhaps come close to the edge of the rocky, flat top without knowing it.

They all sat up.

"Where is that paper bag of scraps?" asked Benny. "Now I'm hungry."

"I have it," said Jessie. "I also have some napkins. Put your hands out and take a napkin, and I will try to divide the breakfast."

She broke the big hamburger into five pieces. Then she got out of her sleeping bag and went down the line putting scraps of roll and one whole roll on each napkin. She gave Mr. Alden his cold coffee. There were four cups on the top of the thermos bottle.

"Tell me when you want a drink of water," she said. "We mustn't waste a drop."

Violet was on one end of the row, and Henry was on the other. They could not see each other because of the fog, but they could hear very well.

Everyone started to eat breakfast. Violet said, "I wouldn't think bread crusts could taste so delicious."

Grandfather said with a laugh, "Nor cold coffee mixed with Coke."

Benny said, "After this, you'll have to put Coke in your coffee instead of sugar."

Henry said, "I certainly hope the fog will lift before lunchtime because we haven't a crumb of food left."

Henry had no sooner said this than the fog lifted. Like magic it entirely disappeared.

"That's the way fog does," said Henry. "And don't forget it can shut down just as fast. Maybe it will come back."

"You're the gloomy one," Jessie said, but she laughed.

"Well," said Mr. Alden, "I don't think it will this time. Look at that sun!"

The whole valley was golden in the bright sunshine. There was not a cloud in the sky.

"Maybe we ought to get ready for the helicopter," said Violet. "We don't want to keep them waiting."

They got their packs ready, rolled up the sleeping bags, and waited.

"Remember when that big rock fell?" said Benny. "I think I really saw a hole, a huge one. Like a cave maybe."

Grandfather said, "You may be sure we will find out. Ah! Here comes the helicopter."

"I guess they know the fog has gone away," said Jessie.

The Aldens saw the helicopter whirring far above them and then slowly coming down. Without a word they all stood behind the hump. This left an open place for the helicopter to land. It came straight down and landed exactly in the middle of the space.

"Straight as a string," said Benny. "Oh, look who's

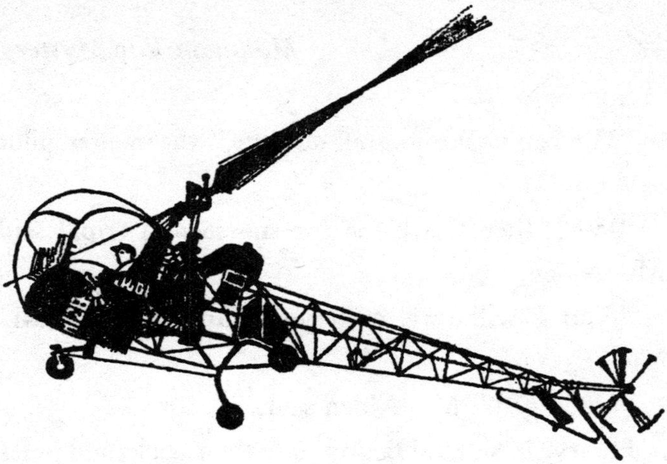

here! It's Mr. Carter!"

Violet cried, "Now where in the world did *he* come from?"

Grandfather smiled.

"Really," said Jessie, "how did he know about us, Grandfather?"

"That will be a good puzzle for you to guess," said Mr. Alden.

"Pooh!" said Benny. "I bet I can tell you exactly what happened. I'll bet you told the ranger to send for Mr. Carter right away if anything happened."

By this time Mr. Carter and a ranger had let down the steps and were coming down.

"We can't take you all at once," the ranger pilot said.

"Well, then, leave me for the second trip," said Mr. Alden.

"And I will stay with you, Grandfather," said Violet.

"Good girl," Mr. Alden said.

Henry, Jessie, and Benny took their packs and poles and sleeping bags. John Carter helped them up the steps into the helicopter.

"We'll be back soon," he said, pulling in the steps.

Sure enough, in a short time the helicopter was back for Grandfather and Violet.

Grandfather asked the pilot to hover over Old Flat Top. There was the hole that Benny thought he saw when the step fell.

"Look, Violet, there's the hole!" shouted Grandfather over the noise of the helicopter.

Down they went to the log store. Even before the plane landed, Violet said, "Grandfather, I see the rangers and some other men, too."

"Yes," Grandfather said, "a man with a camera. I have a feeling the newspaper people heard about the rockslide."

Flashbulbs popped as Mr. Alden and Violet got out of the helicopter. Benny came running up and cried, "Isn't it exciting? A reporter asked me all about what happened."

"Mr. Alden?" a man with a notebook said, coming up to Grandfather. "Your grandson has already told me about his accident. The others told me about his rescue and your night on Old Flat Top. May I ask if you plan to stay here longer?"

"The large hole that was opened when the rockslide took place interests me," Mr.Alden said. "We may stay to learn more."

Benny was listening hard. "Yes, let's stay," he exclaimed. "And you remember that light we saw—"

Before he could say anything more, Mr. Alden told the reporter, "Yes, I think you can say we will be here for a few days. And now we need to get some food. You probably know we had a pretty odd breakfast."

"Thank you," the reporter said, "I understand." He closed his notebook and left with the cameraman.

"Benny," Mr. Alden said, "I didn't think that the reporter needed to know about what we saw during the night. Not until we know more about it ourselves."

A ranger was standing nearby and Henry turned to him. "I have a question, sir. When it was dark, we all saw a very faint light quite deep in the woods. We thought somebody might be in trouble, but the light didn't move. Do you know anything about this?"

"Yes, we do," said one of the rangers. "An old Indian lives there, the last of the tribe. Perfectly harmless. Just wants to live alone and be let alone. Every month I take over some flour, salt, sugar, and tea and a few canned things. Then I bring back sweet grass baskets in trade. They sell like hot cakes—I haven't one left."

Henry asked, "Could I drive the car as far as the house?"

"No. You can go a little way into the woods. Then

you have to walk about a quarter of a mile. The path is easy to follow," the ranger answered.

Mr. Alden came up. He said, "I think we will drive over. My grandchildren are much interested."

John Carter said, "I have my car. I can take Benny and Violet."

Jessie said, "Fine. But we need some lunch. Let's get some food from the store here and then go."

Grandfather agreed and let Jessie plan to get what was needed. "We can eat in the woods before we go up the trail," she said.

The Aldens were soon on their way, Henry driving in the lead. When they had driven as far as they could into the woods, Henry and Mr. Carter parked the cars.

Lunch was quickly eaten because everyone was so curious about the Indian in the woods.

Benny called back, "When we get there, do you think it is all right to knock on the door?"

"I should think so," said Henry. "What else can we do? We want to go in and meet him, don't we? The ranger said he was perfectly harmless."

Soon they saw a small gray house with a large vegetable garden. A stone step was at the front door. Benny knocked.

There was a soft sound of feet and the door opened. There stood a very tall Indian woman who held her head like a queen.

For once Benny did not know what to say. Mr. Alden stepped forward quickly and said, "I hope we are not bothering you. My grandchildren saw your light from Old Flat Top. They were afraid you were in trouble."

The old Indian woman bowed her head a little, opened the door wide, and said, "Please come in."

CHAPTER 4

Lovan's Story

The family was so surprised to find an Indian woman instead of a man that no one said anything.

The room they looked into had two chairs and a couch. On a table lay an Indian basket that was not yet finished. Bunches of sweet grass were hung up to dry. The room was sweet with the smell of the grass.

"Sit down," said the Indian woman. She took the rocking chair, and Mr. Alden sat in the other chair. Mr. Carter sat on the couch and the others sat on the floor.

Still no one had said a word. Then Benny, who was nearest the Indian woman, spoke. He said, "That man is my grandfather, James Alden. John Carter is sitting on the couch. I am Benny and there is my brother Henry and my sisters, Jessie and Violet."

The old woman said, "My name is Lovan Dixon. I am almost ninety years old."

"Well!" exclaimed Benny.

Jessie said, "We were on Flat Top all night and saw your light. We were worried thinking somebody might be in trouble."

"You are very kind," said the woman. "Why were you on Flat Top? Did you have an accident?"

"Yes, *I* did," said Benny. "When I was coming down, the first step broke away. But I don't think about that any more. Grandfather said there was no use in it."

The Indian woman turned to Mr. Alden. "He was right," she said. "I heard all the rocks coming down like thunder. I was worried about you. I saw your fire all night."

Violet looked at the old Indian and asked, "Is anything wrong?"

"Not now," said the woman.

Then Benny cried, "Do you really want to live all alone here?"

"Yes, child," said Lovan Dixon. "I do want to. I do not like living in a town. Too many people laugh at Indian ways. I like to live alone."

Violet and Jessie looked around at the house. It was neat and clean. The old woman's gray hair was as smooth as silk. Her strong old face was deeply wrinkled.

Benny shouted, "Those people were mean. I'd like to tell them so."

"You are a kind boy. There is no need to bother with anyone. I like it here. I love the woods. I am the last of my people. My tribe always lived here and the government gave these woods to my tribe long ago. The woods go to the other side of Flat Top."

Now Grandfather spoke, "But I have a feeling that something is bothering you. Won't you tell us?"

The old woman did not speak for a time and it was very quiet in her little house. Then she said, "I hear that the woods will be cut over for lumber and I will lose my land."

Nodding, John Carter said, "It could be true, Miss Dixon. Many times, I am sorry to say, our government has forgotten its promises to the Indians."

Mr. Alden said, "From this minute on do not worry any more. I know a man who will find out who owns this land. He will buy it himself if he has to. You may use it as long as you live, Miss Dixon."

"Please say 'Lovan,' " said the Indian woman with a bow.

"Lovan," said Benny at once because he liked the sound of the name. "When that step gave way on Old Flat Top, I thought I saw a big hole behind it. Do you think that was really true?"

Lovan folded her arms and sat for a long time with bowed head. There was not a sound. After awhile she drew a long breath and said, "I trust you. Let me tell you a story. Years ago my grandfather told it to me,

and he heard it from his grandfather. You ask about a hole, child. I believe there is a cave."

For a minute Lovan did not say anything more. Then she went on, "You understand this happened years ago. There used to be a cave on the other side of

Flat Top, but no cave where you say the hole is. In those days you couldn't get up the mountain by your trail, but you could get up on the other side. Flat Top didn't have such a flat top at that time."

Every eye was on the old Indian woman. They hoped she would go on, and she did.

"The story goes that a Frenchman who was a friend of the King of France ran away to America to live. There was a war in France and he escaped. He was shot accidently right near here. My great-grandfather, Running Deer, hid him and took care of him until he died. The Frenchman had a great leather bag with things in it which he expected to sell. But when he died, he gave the bag to my great-grandfather for taking care of him."

"What was in the bag?" cried Benny. Lovan smiled at Benny. "I never knew," she said. "My great-grandfather died without telling anyone what was in it. But my grandfather thought that his father hid the bag in that old cave."

"Why didn't he go up and find it?" asked Benny.

Henry said, "Benny, you are asking too many questions."

Lovan smiled a little. She said, "I don't mind. Nobody has ever dared before. Something happened to that mountain and the rocks moved and closed the cave. It looked as if it had been squashed together. That was when Flat Top became flat."

Mr. Carter said, "Didn't anyone try to dig the cave out?"

"No, the rocks were too heavy. Besides the climb was too steep."

Jessie said slowly, "If that bag was ever found, wouldn't it belong to you?"

Lovan bowed again. "Yes," she said. "I am the last of the tribe and my grandfather told me it was mine."

"Wouldn't you expect to get it then," asked Henry, "if somebody found it?"

"I don't know," said Lovan. "I have lost many things."

Violet said, "Do you suppose the hole Benny found

is a sort of back door to that cave?"

"I have no doubt of it," said Lovan.

Mr. Alden said, "Don't worry any more about anything. I myself will see that you get what is yours."

Lovan said, "I am grateful to you. All I have left now is this house and my garden and my front step."

"What about your front step?" asked Mr. Alden.

"Come and see," said Lovan. "You must go down my step and watch."

She followed them out with a cup of water in her hand. They watched her as she poured the water slowly into some hollows in the step.

"A big, enormous claw!" cried Benny. "It is almost as long as the step."

"A dinosaur track!" shouted Henry. "I've seen one at college."

Grandfather said, "Where did you get this? It is certainly a big piece of red sandstone."

"Yes," said Lovan. "It came from the ledge right over there. My grandfather thought it was the track of a big magic bird. They called it a thunderbird track."

Benny laughed. "That's a car," he said.

Mr. Carter said, "They named the car for the magic bird."

"I suppose you know," said Jessie, "that a museum would like your step."

"But I want my doorstep," said Lovan.

"And you shall keep it," said Mr. Alden. "The man who buys your woods would want you to have it. And now I think we should go. Thank you for everything."

"But we'll be back," said Benny. He gave Lovan a great smile, the kind only Benny could give.

CHAPTER 5

More Plans

When the Aldens were in the car, Violet said, "We can see right through you, Grandfather. You are the man who is going to buy the woods, aren't you?"

"Of course," said Grandfather, smiling at her. "What better thing could we do for Lovan? She will feel free, and don't forget, I will have a fine woodlot. John, you attend to that for me, will you?"

Mr. Carter laughed. "I was already planning my first step."

Henry said, "I don't see how we can go home and leave this whole thing, Grandfather. What do you think of staying at a motel for a few days?"

"All right," said Mr. Alden, "that's a good idea. We can ask the ranger where the nearest motel is."

Benny said, "Three rooms would be right for us. One for the girls, one for us boys, and one for Grandfather."

Turning to John Carter, Mr. Alden said, "It's settled that we'll stay here. I think you had better drive back to look after business details."

Everyone waved as Mr. Carter drove off. At the log store, the Aldens found the ranger they knew.

"Did you find Lovan Dixon at home?" he asked.

"Oh, yes," Jessie said. "What a wonderful old woman she is!"

"You will never believe it," said the ranger, "but that Indian woman, ninety years old, has to walk five miles to the swamp to get the sweet grass and five miles back. Quite a walk for ninety. We sell the baskets just as fast as we get them."

"I'd like a sewing basket like that," Jessie said, "and so would Violet."

"I think Miss Dixon would make you some if you asked," the ranger said. "But if you ask her first, don't try to pay for them. It will be a gift, you can be sure. She gave one to my wife, so I know. I tried to pay her and she was very much hurt."

Now Grandfather spoke, "Do you happen to know if Dr. Percy Osgood and his men are working somewhere in this neighborhood? I have an idea Percy would be interested in the cave Benny found by accident."

"Yes, we saw the cave from the helicopter. The rocks were huge that fell away to leave it open," one of the rangers said. "Look out of the door and you can see the pile that rolled down the mountain."

Indeed there was a pile of rocks of all sizes, perhaps ten feet high. "And I am glad it did not turn into a bigger rockslide," the ranger said. "I know Dr. Osgood is not too far off. Let me make some calls and I will get his telephone number for you."

"Good," said Mr. Alden. "Let's find that motel. Where is the nearest one?"

"Go back to the main road, turn to the right, and then go about half a mile. That's the nearest motel, and the best one, too."

"How lucky we are!" said Benny. "Things seem to happen just right for us."

The family went out to the station wagon and Henry started the car. They drove away, waving at the ranger.

"We'll be back soon," cried Benny.

"Perhaps not until tomorrow," called Grandfather with a wink.

"The kids are pretty tired, I guess," shouted the ranger.

"I wasn't tired at all until he said that," said Jessie, "and now I guess I am."

"I guess I am, too," said Grandfather. "The first thing I will do will be to take a nap."

Henry drove just as the ranger had said. He soon came to a motel. It was a long row of log buildings. At one end there was an office and at the other a restaurant.

"Good," said Jessie. "I shall be glad to have a real dinner. It seems as if we've been gone much longer than two days."

Benny said, "I know just what I'm going to eat, too."

Grandfather said, "Don't tell, then. Keep it for a surprise."

The three motel rooms were just alike. Each had two beds and a bathroom.

Benny said, "Oh, I can hardly wait to wash my hands! It has been two days since I've really washed them!"

"Funny to hear you say that, Ben," said Henry. "I'm going to take a shower the first thing I do."

It did not take long for the Aldens to make themselves at home in their three motel rooms.

"First thing is a shower for me," said Henry.

"I'm next," Benny said. "And after that I'm going to try out that bed."

Violet and Jessie, too, decided to shower and nap. But it was Grandfather who was the first one asleep. There hadn't been much sleep for anyone for two nights.

An hour or so later Benny saw that Henry was awake. He said, "Guess what I'm going to have for dinner."

"You can't keep that secret, Ben, can you?" said Henry. "But wait. They may not have it."

"I never thought of that," said Benny. "I hope they will, because I've got my mind all made up."

At five-thirty nobody could wait any longer. They walked down to the restaurant and found a table for five.

"Too bad Mr. Carter's missing this," said Violet. "I'm going to have roast beef and mashed potatoes and peas!"

"And a fine hot summer diet, too!" said Mr. Alden. "I'll have the same."

Jessie and Henry could not think of anything better, but Benny said, "Corned beef and cabbage! And lots of chili sauce and turnips and carrots!"

How wonderful that meal did taste! The waiter was amused. He watched Benny cut the tender red corned beef as if he were starving.

After the first few bites, Jessie said, "Grandfather, what is the first step that Mr. Carter is going to take?"

"Try to buy the woodlot is first," said Mr. Alden. "Then you all heard the name of Dr. Percy Osgood. He is a great man and an explorer. He has written several books on caves and mountains. He is always interested in any new crack or landslide. I used to know him years ago. He can tell right away whether this hole is interesting or not."

"I bet it is!" cried Benny.

"Well, I won't bet against you," said Grandfather, smiling. "I think it is, too, otherwise I should not have asked the ranger to send for Percy Osgood and let him waste his time."

"Let's stay in the motel until the whole thing is solved," said Benny. "Don't you agree, Grandfather?"

"Yes, my boy," said Mr. Alden, smiling. "I couldn't

tear myself away now for anything."

Henry said, "The great question is, is it a cave or is it just a hole?"

Jessie said, "Or is it a cave with something interesting in it or is it a cave with nothing in it?"

Benny was drinking milk now. He said, "I'm going to have bread pudding for dessert."

"I hope you can hold all that food," said Grandfather, looking at him.

"Oh, I can!" said Benny. "I have a hollow leg."

Henry said suddenly, "Grandfather, did you expect an accident on Flat Top?"

"No," said Mr. Alden, "but I never like a place that has only one way to get in and only one way to get out."

That night at about twelve o'clock a man came to the office and took the room next to Henry and Benny. At one o'clock another man took the last room next to the restaurant. But nobody woke up and none of the Alden family knew anything about the two men until the next morning at breakfast.

CHAPTER 6

Back Up the Trail

The Alden family did not get up very early next morning. But when they walked into the dining room they had a surprise. There sat John Carter at a large round table for seven.

"Oh, I'm glad you found us!" shouted Benny.

"I never lost you," said John Carter, getting up. He pulled chairs out for Jessie and Violet and soon they were all chattering at once.

"I thought you might like to see this paper," Mr. Carter said. He unfolded a newspaper to show a headline that read "Rescued by Helicopter."

"Here we are!" Benny said. "And it tells about the rockslide and the hole in Old Flat Top and everything."

"That's right," Mr. Carter said. "How does it feel to read about yourselves in the paper?"

Jessie was looking around at the table, "Who is the seventh place for?" she asked.

Mr. Alden and Mr. Carter looked at each other.

"Then he got here last night?" Mr. Alden asked. "He is not one to waste time."

"Who got here?" Benny asked.

"I'll make a guess," Henry said. "Dr. Osgood?"

"If it is Dr. Osgood—and I'm not saying it is—how do you think he'll look?" asked Grandfather.

Jessie answered, "Oh, I guess he is a tall, large man. He must be strong to climb all these high mountains."

"Yes, that's right," said Mr. Carter. "He must be a very strong man."

Benny said, "If a big tall strong man should come in that door, I should say it would be Dr. Percy Osgood."

Mr. Alden said, "Better order your breakfast, and

not keep the waiter waiting!"

Everyone ordered bacon and eggs and toast and orange juice and milk. Grandfather and Mr. Carter had coffee.

They were all busily eating when the door opened. They looked up. There stood a small man not much taller than Benny or Violet. His hair was pure white and his eyes very sharp and blue. His glasses were pushed up on his forehead. He was surely not young, but he walked quickly over to Grandfather to shake hands.

"Good to see you again," said Grandfather. "You came soon. My grandchildren can hardly wait."

"That's the way I feel," said Dr. Osgood, looking at each one in turn. "I would start working without eating any breakfast, only I have learned to eat when I can. One doesn't get so tired."

He sat down and ordered the same breakfast as the rest.

Benny asked, "Have you made any plans about what you will do first, Dr. Osgood?"

"Oh, yes! I made them on the train as I came here. A cave isn't usually so high on a mountain as this one. We have to build a staging first. The staging has to be strong to hold the workmen and the machines. It will take three days at least to make that."

"Three days!" cried Benny.

"You'll find, young man, that three days will go by

just like that!" He snapped his fingers. "Making a staging is interesting. If you feel like climbing the mountain again, you can all sit below and watch the work."

"Oh, yes, we'd like that," said Jessie. "I was afraid we wouldn't see anything."

"Well," said Dr. Osgood with a twinkle, "what would be the good of that? The very people who found the cave not watching the workmen! No, sir! Not possible!"

"I'll drive you over after breakfast," said Henry. "Whenever you say."

"Thank you," said Dr. Osgood. "I accept."

As they left the table, Grandfather said, "By the way, Percy, I have a story about the hole in Flat Top that I'd like to tell you. Why don't you stop in my room?"

Dr. Osgood's eyebrows shot up. But all he said was, "Do I smell a bit of a mystery? Now let me see. Is it pirate gold or an Indian grave?"

"Well, those guesses are good. But I would rather

talk where we are alone. This just might be important to someone."

In about half an hour the Aldens and Dr. Osgood were getting into the station wagon. When they arrived at the loghouse store, there was quite a crowd of men and women and children standing around.

The ranger said to Dr. Osgood, "Two of your men have already gone up the trail. Do you want me to go first and show you the way?"

"Thank you, no," said Dr. Osgood. "I think I can find my way. I'm sure it will be full of rocks brought down by the landslide. You Aldens follow me!"

The Aldens went up the trail after the spry little man, but they could not see him.

Mr. Alden said, "Now it takes three hours to get to the top. We'd better not hurry. We're not used to it. I'll go first, then Violet. That will slow you down, I guess."

"That's OK," said Benny.

But it was not Mr. Alden and Violet who slowed them down. It was the rocks. Many of them had come down with the landslide. As Henry climbed over a rock he cried, "See how different some of these rocks are? Some are sharp, just broken off the day we came down. But look at those huge ones, perfectly smooth! I'm sure those were left here by a glacier."

"Right," said Grandfather. "This is a fine place to study rocks."

As they climbed slowly, Henry turned around and said to Jessie, "Did you notice that crowd at the store?"

"I certainly did," said Jessie. "I suppose they came to see the excitement."

Henry asked in a low voice, "Did you see what I saw? An Indian boy?"

"Yes, I did. He didn't look very happy, did he? And when I looked at him, he turned around and hid behind another man."

There was a pause while they climbed further. Then Jessie said, "I thought the ranger said Lovan was the only Indian around here."

"That's what I thought, too," said Henry.

CHAPTER 7

A Stranger

Henry and Jessie did not say any more about the Indian boy, but they did not forget him. Once in awhile they both wondered where he came from and why he was there. They also wondered why he did not want to be seen.

There was plenty to think about while they were still climbing. In some places the path was almost blocked by the fallen rocks. They had to climb over them or walk around them.

Benny called back, "It's lucky nobody was on this trail when these rocks came down!"

Grandfather said, "I was just going to say we should be ready to dodge if any more come down."

"I think somebody is behind us," said Henry. "We'd better be careful not to send any more down on top of him."

"I *hope* somebody is behind us," said Mr. Alden with a laugh. "Otherwise we'll have no lunch. John Carter is supposed to bring up enough lunch for us and the workmen and Dr. Osgood."

"Well, he'll have a heavy load," said Benny. "That will be lunch for nine people!"

"Don't worry about John Carter," said Grandfather. "He'll manage."

When they were quite near the top, they heard noises. It sounded like chopping and pounding, and that was exactly what it was. The two workmen were soon seen chopping down bushes and small trees to the left of the path. There were no trees or bushes near the top; there it was all rock.

The workmen had cleared a spot that looked like a good place to sit and watch what was going on.

There was some lumber, a strong ladder, and a long, flat plank. The plank had been placed near the opening to the cave and was held down with rocks.

Dr. Osgood was standing on the plank and bending over to look into the dark hole.

Benny said, "I guess Dr. Osgood couldn't wait."

The explorer held a bright light in his hand. His glasses were pulled down and he was too busy to notice the Aldens.

Grandfather sat down on the dry grass. He said, "I think Dr. Osgood wants to see first what kind of a hole it is. Just see whether it will be worth exploring or not."

"Oh, dear!" cried Benny. "I hope it turns out to be worth exploring. Wouldn't it be awful if we had to give up and go home?"

"I don't think we will," said Henry. "Look at him now."

Dr. Osgood had both arms and his head in the hole. The Aldens could see only a pair of legs.

Just then Dr. Osgood looked up from the hole and

turned half around. He called to the workmen, but the Aldens could not hear what he said. However, the workmen did and called back, "Very good, sir!" They were used to working with Dr. Osgood.

Then Dr. Osgood started to climb down to talk to Grandfather. He sat down beside him and pushed up his glasses again.

"Well, Percy, what's the good word?" asked Grandfather.

"A very good word," said Dr. Osgood, nodding. He wiped his face with a big red handerchief. "Now, you know I never saw Old Flat Top before it was flattened." He smiled at the young people. "But I have good reason to think the first cave was on the back of the mountain. Then something happened like a small earthquake. The back was pushed down and closed up that hole. But this front end of the cave was *not* squashed. So it is just the same as it has been for many years."

Benny said, "Then this front hole is really the back of the cave."

"Right," said Dr. Osgood. "You'll be a cave-digger some day."

"Are you going to blast?" asked Benny.

"No, I don't think so. We can drill as far as we need to. The other end is completely closed, they say. However, we'll wait and see. Hello, here comes my help."

"Oh, I thought it was *my* help," said Grandfather, "with some lunch."

"It's both," said Henry, who could see the trail. He looked down. Two more workmen were dragging a heavy load of lumber. John Carter was behind, a large knapsack on his back.

Henry said, "Dr. Osgood, what did you see when you put the light in the cave?"

"Well, I could see about ten feet with the light," said Dr. Osgood. "The hole grows larger. I should say if we crawled in about fifteen feet we could stand up. It surely has not been touched by human hands for about two hundred years. Maybe a bit less; maybe a bit more. However, I saw no treasures. You must be willing to explore and find *nothing*. That's why this job takes patience. Lots of my work goes for nothing. Wasted."

"I wouldn't like that," said Benny.

"No, I can see that you wouldn't," said Dr. Osgood.

He got up quickly from the ground and climbed up to the workmen. He began to put blue chalk marks on many of the rocks.

When he had gone, Grandfather said quietly, "Did any of you notice an Indian boy in the crowd?"

"Yes!" they all cried.

Henry said, "We thought Lovan told us that she was the last Indian around here. That surprised us."

"Maybe she doesn't know about this boy," said Mr. Alden.

John Carter sat down with the family. He said, "I did try to talk with the boy. But I had to order the lunch. I couldn't take enough time. But I will."

"Good!" said Mr. Alden. "Maybe he doesn't live here anyway. Maybe he heard of this work on Flat Top."

"He heard fast, then," said Benny.

"Well, news travels fast," said Grandfather thoughtfully.

"I hope he won't bother Lovan," said Violet.

"Well, after we get down we'll see that he doesn't," said Mr. Alden. "Right now, we are trying to find Lovan's treasure."

"Wouldn't it be awful if somebody stole it last night?" exclaimed Benny.

"Well, it is possible," said John Carter. "They had all night, if they were good climbers and worked quietly."

CHAPTER 8

The First Find

"Couldn't we go up that ladder," asked Benny, "and look in the hole?"

"Not yet, young man," said Dr. Osgood. He pushed up his glasses. "We don't want any more accidents. When we get the staging done, it will be safe for any of you to get up to the cave."

Mr. Alden said, "Percy, the old Indian woman Lovan told us that her great-great-grandfather hid that leather bag in a cave. Now suppose this was the cave. Would that be near this door or near the opening in the other side, do you think?"

"I should say he crawled in and hid it as far back as he could," said Dr. Osgood.

Benny said, "That would mean the leather bag could be right under our noses! I hope they will get that staging done fast. I can hardly wait! Can you, Mr. Carter?"

Mr. Carter said, "No, I can hardly wait, either. But right now I am hungry. Aren't you all hungry?"

"Always!" said Henry and Jessie together.

"Well, then, how about a bit of lunch?" said John Carter. "You've had a three-hour climb, and we all need food. And you should see the lunch!"

"Oh, we'll never eat all this food!" Jessie said as she watched the lunch being unpacked.

"Don't forget, it is for the workmen, too," said Dr. Osgood. "And me!"

Then Henry noticed that Benny was sitting still and saying nothing.

"What's the matter, Ben?"

"Well, I simply can't decide which sandwiches I like best!" said Benny. "I like them all best."

"Shut your eyes and point, then," said Mr. Carter.

Benny did so. He was pointing at the cheeseburgers.

"That's exactly what I do like best, really!" he cried. "Cheeseburgers!"

"I thought you didn't know," laughed Violet.

"Yes, I thought so, too," said Benny. "And I just love to dunk hard-boiled eggs!" He opened his salt and pepper and "dunked" his egg in the salt as he spoke. Then he bit off a huge bite.

"Delicious!" he said.

Everyone agreed. The piles of sandwiches went down very fast. But there were plenty for the workmen when Mr. Alden called them to lunch. When the workmen sat down, the Alden family waited on them. Henry gave them hot coffee. Violet passed the pickles. Mr. Carter got out the cold drinks. Jessie gave each one an egg and salt. Benny sat down with them and had another sandwich. He said, "You haven't really got very far on the staging, have you?"

"No," said the head man. "It takes three days. You see a staging must not fall. And it has to rest somewhere. It takes time to make a place to hold it."

"Don't you keep wishing that you could take time off and look in the cave?" asked Benny.

"Yes," said a man. "But if we do, the staging has to wait, and it takes that much longer to finish it. Dr. Percy has had a look. That's enough for me. He thinks it is worth while, so I'm not wasting my time."

Henry said to Dr. Osgood, "What do you think could be in the lost bag? A French nobleman expected to sell whatever it was for enough money to live here. So it must be worth something."

"It could be jewelry," said Dr. Osgood. "French noblemen often had to sell jewels to keep alive. It could be gold coins or silver. It could be silver candlesticks or vases or mirrors or spoons. I don't know."

"I know you, Percy!" said Mr. Alden. "You're not really interested in that leather bag, are you?"

"Well, no, not much," said Dr. Osgood. "I always hope to find something important in a cave."

"What could be more important than Lovan's treasure?" cried Benny.

"Well, you're right, boy, if you are thinking mostly of Lovan. But for the whole country, stones could be more important. They are to me." He threw his head back and tried not to laugh.

Grandfather shook his finger at his old friend. "You're up to something, Percy! Have you found something already?"

"I suppose I shall have to show it to you," said Dr. Osgood. "At first I thought I'd put it back and let Benny find it. But Benny wouldn't like that if he found it out."

"No, I wouldn't," said Benny.

"Here it is," said Dr. Osgood. He took a flat stone out of the biggest pocket of his overalls. It was about six inches long. He gave it to Henry, not Benny. "Take care!" he said.

"A fossil," said Henry. He took the stone carefully in both hands. It was one flat stone, but it was split down the middle.

"Take off the cover," said Dr. Osgood. "Careful now!"

Henry lifted the top half and they all bent over to look.

"A little fish!" cried Benny.

"Yes, a fossil fish," said Dr. Osgood. "It is millions of years old."

"What kind of a fish?" asked Benny. He was sure Dr. Osgood knew everything.

"I don't know," said Dr. Osgood. "You may be sure that many people will study this fossil. See the backbone? Every little bone shows on both halves."

"Does that mean that once this mountain top was under water?" asked Jessie.

"Yes," said Dr. Osgood, nodding, "and this is the proof. I'd rather find this than ten leather bags."

Dr. Osgood said, "And now you'll be surprised to hear this. I think you had better start down the mountain. The weather doesn't look too fine to me."

"It looks beautiful to me," said Benny, looking at the deep blue sky. "But of course you would be right. Are you coming, too?"

"No, I'll stay. I'll keep my head man and we'll come

down later in the helicopter."

Jessie did not have to be told twice. She was already packing the things.

Three hours later they reached the store. They all went in, and Mr. Carter said to the ranger, "Did you see the Indian boy this morning in the crowd?"

"Yes, he is new around here. Before I had time to talk to him, he had gone."

"Gone!" cried everyone.

"Yes, gone. And what's more, he's still gone. Nobody around here ever saw him before. And nobody knew how he got here."

"That's very funny," said Henry. "I should think somebody would have spoken to him. There was such a crowd. Would you guess he was up to no good?"

"Well," said the ranger. He stopped. Then he went on, "We know nothing about him. He may be lost and need help. That's really why we're going to find him, come what may."

CHAPTER 9

Caught in the Rain

Mr. Alden walked around the store looking at everything. There were no Indian baskets left. He said, "Let's go to see Lovan again."

"Don't get caught in the storm," said a ranger.

"Storm? It looks pleasant to me," said Benny.

"Well, you get to know the weather around these mountains," said the ranger. "I was glad to see you come down so early. Dr. Osgood will be all right. He knows the weather, too."

What they did not know was that snow had suddenly begun to cover the top of Old Flat Top. Dr.

Osgood and his workmen were just running to get the things packed on the helicopter to take off in a hurry.

The Aldens piled into the station wagon and drove down to Lovan Dixon's. The sky was still blue with hardly a cloud. It was very warm. They found Lovan hoeing in her flower garden next to the house.

"I want to get the earth stirred up before it rains," she said to her visitors.

Grandfather laughed. "You think it is going to rain, too," he said.

"Oh, yes," said Lovan. "But come in."

"What beautiful flowers!" cried Violet. "Every one is such a lovely color."

Lovan looked at the eager little girl. She said, "Little Violet, you take these scissors and cut a big bunch of every flower you like. Don't be afraid to pick a lot. They like to be picked. They blossom all the more."

Mr. Alden smiled. But he had come on business, so he was glad to go into the house and ask questions.

"I wonder if you ever heard of an Indian boy

around here about high school age?" he asked.

"No," Lovan shook her head. "I am the only Indian left around here. All my brothers died, and my only sister died. She had a daughter, but she died, too."

"Didn't your sister's daughter have any children?"

"I did hear that she had a son, but that baby died when she did. They had moved into Maine with the Maine Indians by then."

"What was that baby's name?" asked Henry.

"I don't know. We had quarreled and I never did learn the baby's name."

Mr. Carter said, "We saw a young Indian boy this morning. He looked unhappy and seemed to be afraid. He hid behind the crowd, and now he has disappeared."

"Oh, dear!" said Lovan.

"We'll find him," Benny said.

"How?" asked Lovan. "I thought you said he ran away."

"Yes, he did. But he never could get away with Mr. Carter after him, and the rangers, and Grandfather."

Just then Violet came in with her flowers. They were beautiful—pink and white roses, old-fashioned sweet pinks, yellow daisies, lavender heliotrope, larkspur, and sweet peas.

"Let's go right home and put them in water!" Violet said. "I can't let them fade!" She made a pretty picture standing in the door with her brown hair, pink cheeks, and the lovely flowers.

"Soon," said Grandfather. "Just one more question and then we'll go. Why did your family leave you?"

"I left *them*," said Lovan. "I wanted to go to school and nobody else did. They called me stuck-up because I could read and write. I loved school. There were children of all ages. When I was older, I helped the teacher with the little ones. I taught them the good things of Indian life. I taught them to make baskets and beadwork and moccasins. The children were very good at making up designs—even the little ones."

"Good!" said Grandfather. "Someone must do that, or we'll lose all the beautiful things that nobody can make as well as the Indian."

"It's too bad you don't know anything about this strange Indian boy," said Henry.

Lovan said slowly, "If he is from my family, his grandmother's name would be Susan."

"That's something to go on," said Henry.

"Come on, everyone," said Mr. Alden. "Violet wants to go."

"I don't want to go," said Violet, smiling, "I just

want to put the flowers in water."

As the Aldens left Lovan's cottage they felt a cool wind. Clouds were beginning to sweep across the sky. The day that had been so sunny was suddenly very dark. A storm was brewing.

Mr. Alden said, "We will go to the motel first and then go and talk to the rangers."

"I'll stay at the motel," said Violet. "I'll put the flowers in water before supper. There must be some vases someplace."

Everyone knew that Violet was perfectly happy arranging flowers. The rest of the family went back to the store. There was only one man there. He was not a ranger.

"Where is everybody?" asked Mr. Alden.

"They've all gone off in their jeeps to find an Indian boy. I'm keeping the store."

Grandfather nodded. "They don't waste much time, I see. The rainstorm will soon be here. I only wish we could have gone with them."

"Listen!" said Jessie. "Dr. Osgood's storm!"

The rain blew a few small spatters in at the open door. Then it came down like a sheet of water. It simply poured.

"Too bad the rangers started out," said Benny. "They'll get soaking wet."

The man said, "They knew it was going to rain. They all wore raincoats. I think they thought the Indian boy would be easier to find in the rain."

"How?" asked Benny.

The man shrugged. "I don't know. They know more about finding people than I do. They do it all the time."

Then in the pouring rain Dr. Osgood and his workman came in the door.

"Oh, everything is happening at once!" cried Benny. "Here come the jeeps!"

Dr. Osgood came in at exactly the same time as a ranger jumped down from a jeep. Then another ranger jumped out. Then another person jumped down. He had no raincoat and no hat. Water streamed down over his face. He kept his eyes down.

CHAPTER 10

David Explains

When the rangers led the Indian boy into the store, Jessie was near the door. Quickly she put her hand on the boy's shoulder. "Don't be afraid," she said. "We want to help you."

The boy did not look up, but he pushed back his wet hair.

A ranger said, "This boy belongs in Maine. When he heard about Flat Top on a radio program he begged rides and got here in no time. He's interested in the cave, but so far I don't know why."

They all sat down. The boy was on a wooden chair. His clothes dripped on the floor.

The chief ranger took off his raincoat and sat down at a desk. He said to the boy, "This is a very small village, son. We always notice any strangers. We want to know why you came here, what you expect to find, and also why you ran away. You will save time if you tell the exact truth. If you tell a lie, we will find it out. First, what is your name?"

The boy waited a minute. "David Walker," he said.

"That's not an Indian name," said the ranger.

"No, my Indian name is David Walking-by-Night."

"A nice name," whispered Jessie to Henry. "But Lovan's last name is Dixon."

The ranger went on, "Why were you interested in Flat Top?"

David Walking-by-Night drew a long breath. He seemed very tired, but he seemed to be telling the truth.

"I was born in Maine," he said. "But I don't belong in Maine. My mother came from another tribe down here. She told me stories about Flat Top."

"What stories?" shouted Benny.

David looked at Benny. He did not smile. He said, "The stories may not be true. But one story is about

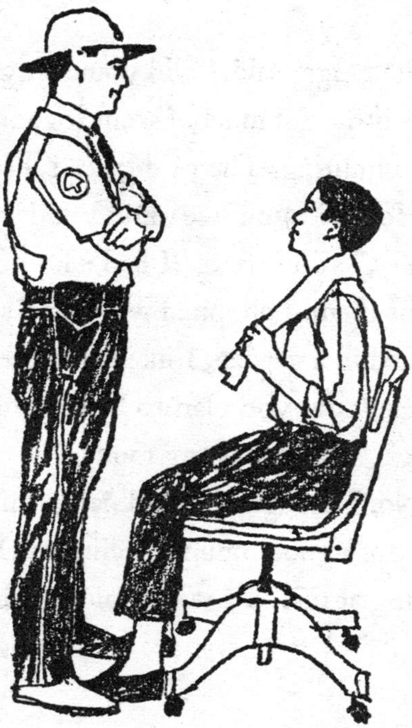

some treasure that belongs to my tribe. I thought I might get it sometime."

The ranger said, "That treasure would belong to your mother's people first, wouldn't it?"

"Yes, but they are all dead long ago. I'm the only one left in that tribe. My mother is dead, too."

Nobody spoke for a minute. It was not hard to guess that this boy without a family had no one to care about him.

The ranger said, "Did you ever go to school, son?"

"A little, not much. I went for a few weeks and then I'd go hunting. Then I'd go to school for awhile."

"How did you live? Did you have a job?"

"Yes," said David. "I had a lot of jobs. I didn't like any of them. I chopped wood and shoveled snow and worked in a garden. I liked that the best."

"How did you plan to live down here?" asked the ranger. "Have you any money?"

"No. I thought I could carry things up the mountain. I'm a good mountain climber. But everyone kept looking at me, so I was afraid and ran."

Mr. Alden spoke for the first time. He said, "Now, David, I am beginning to make some guesses. If I am right, I think a new life is open to you if you want to take it. Right now I know you are tired. We have heard enough for tonight."

David looked at Mr. Alden and no one needed to tell the boy that he had found a friend. He said, "Thank you, sir."

Benny said, "I can guess as well as Grandfather. Can't we take David to the motel and get him some food and dry clothes?"

"There is an extra bed in my room," Mr. Carter said. "David can sleep there. How about it, David?"

The boy nodded, but Grandfather said, "Let's be sure our plan checks with the ranger." Then he said, "Is this plan all right with you, sir? I'll take this boy with me and take good care of him. I'll see that he comes to no harm."

"Perfectly all right," said the ranger. He had learned that John Carter was an ex-F.B.I. man. "The boy hasn't done anything wrong."

"We'd better go right along," said Jessie. "David needs something to eat."

Mr. Carter said, "I'll take Dave and Benny and Jessie in my car. Henry, you take Mr. Alden and Dr. Osgood."

The two cars soon arrived at the motel. Benny had chattered most of the way. Jessie and Mr. Carter had talked pleasantly. But the Indian boy had not said a word.

Henry said, "The first thing we'll do is find dry clothes for you while you're taking a shower."

Henry went at once to his clothes drawer. He got out dry clothes for David. They were all too big, but they had to do. Benny's shoes were just right for him.

When everyone was washed and dressed they met in the dining room.

"He's a good looking boy," thought Violet when she met him.

"Let's all have hot soup," said Mr. Alden. "I'm just as tired as David is."

John Carter thought to himself, "That boy has not eaten anything for a good many hours. I hope he doesn't faint."

David looked first to see how Henry ate his soup, and then he did the same.

"He cares," thought John Carter. "He wants to do things right." He had a question to ask, but he waited until the soup was gone and a tiny bit of color came into the boy's face.

Then he said, "You know, David, we hear there is a big leather bag in some cave, with treasures in it. It belonged to an Indian who died long ago. Have you heard this story?"

"Yes, sir!" said David eagerly. "I heard more than that. I heard that a foreign man had it first. He gave it to an Indian who was afraid somebody would follow him, so he got a big bundle of corn, and hid the bag under the corn."

All this time Dr. Osgood had been eating soup and smiling to himself. He waited until the roast chicken dinner came. Then he cleared his throat and said,

"Ahem!" just to be sure that everyone was looking at him.

"I just want to say," he began, "that all this is very important and interesting. But nobody has said a single word about Old Flat Top!"

"Tell us!" they all shouted.

"Well, the staging is all done," said Dr. Osgood. "And I crawled inside for twenty-five feet."

"Any bag?" yelled Benny.

"Well, no," said Dr. Osgood, smiling. "There are some things right on the floor of the cave that are very interesting to me. The walls seem to be just big smooth rocks."

Benny said, "Oh, Dr. Osgood, there must be some place where something could be hidden."

"You'll have to see for yourself," Dr. Osgood said. "Maybe your sharp young eyes will see something my old ones missed."

CHAPTER 11

Benny Finds the Way

Dr. Osgood promised the family that they could all explore the cave in the morning. They went to bed feeling very much excited.

Mr. Carter and David talked awhile before they went to sleep.

"David, what's on your mind? What are you afraid of?" Mr. Carter asked.

There was a long silence. At last David said, "I climbed Flat Top the night before you did. I heard about the rockslide and the hole on a news program, so I came down from Maine fast. I thought I was the last Indian to know about the treasure and it could be mine. I was going to take it, and no fuss."

"Now supposing this treasure was yours and somebody else found it. Didn't you think they would give it to you?"

"No, I didn't think they would."

"Well, I don't really blame you," said Mr. Carter. "Were you afraid of the rangers after you climbed Flat Top? Did you think they knew your secret?"

"I wasn't sure. But I thought they wouldn't believe anything I said. I didn't make a sound, either. I can walk through the woods and up the mountain without making any noise. But I thought they found out somehow. They looked at me so funny that I hid in the woods."

"Nothing to eat?"

"No. I didn't dare take anything with me. I thought later I would find out about any treasure, but the rangers found me first."

"Is that all?" asked John Carter.

"Yes, sir," said David.

"You couldn't get up to the cave? You didn't even look in?"

"No, I couldn't. There wasn't any way to get close. I just saw the hole. Then I had to come down."

"Dave, I want you to understand the Aldens are your friends," said John Carter. "They are fine people. They want to help you. You must not let them down."

"No," said David. "I like them. They wouldn't cheat me, I know."

Everyone was up early next morning. They ate breakfast and then drove to the foot of Flat Top.

Soon everyone was climbing up the old trail again. Benny came right after Dr. Osgood. The doctor did not climb so fast today. All of a sudden he looked around at Benny.

"Young man, don't get your hopes up on that treasure. I didn't see a single place where it might be. We are going still further into the cave, but I don't think I missed it."

"Oh," said Benny. "Lovan will be disappointed. I was so sure it was right here. That's where I would have put it, just as far back as I could. And that would be the front now."

"Well, you're not an Indian, son, and this isn't two hundred years ago. Maybe the man had other ideas."

"I hope not," said Benny. "Just for Lovan's sake."

David was behind Benny. "Did you say Lovan?" he said. "I have heard that name. But she is dead."

"Our Lovan isn't dead," said Benny. "She is ninety years old, though. And she is the one who told us about the treasure."

"My grandmother told me everyone was dead but me," said David.

Benny said, "Do you know your grandmother's first name?"

"Yes, it was Susan."

Henry was right behind David and he heard the name. He said, "Lovan had a sister Susan. It looks to me as if you are Lovan Dixon's grandnephew. That would be great, because you could help her. She is getting old now, and she lives all alone."

"What is she like?" asked David.

"She's swell!" said Benny.

The family climbed and climbed. It was almost noon when they reached the staging. The workmen were there. They had put a strong light inside the cave for Dr. Osgood. They were just finishing the wiring.

"I'll go first," said Dr. Osgood. "And you can all follow me. First you have to crawl in, but soon you can stand up. You'll see."

The cave was bigger than the Aldens had expected. There was plenty of room for everyone. Dr. Osgood began at once to chip out another fossil. This time it was a fern, an important find. The fern told him how old the cave was.

Benny watched him for a few minutes. Then he went back and crawled to the door of the cave. David went, too.

"Let's see if these stones can possibly be moved," said Benny. He looked at one side of the opening. The big rocks came out to make a large square.

"That looks like a chimney," said David.

"So it does!" cried Benny. "It looks like a closet

in a corner of a room." He stuck his head out of the cave and called to a workman, "Hey! Please come and look. Do you think anything could be hidden there?"

The man laughed. He said, "We can find out." He got a small crowbar and a hammer and went to work. Soon he said, "You're right, Sonny. These rocks don't belong here. They were moved here."

Benny didn't like to be called Sonny, but this was no time to say so. Henry came over to watch. Then he called the girls and Mr. Alden and Mr. Carter.

The workman said, "When this stone falls, there will be clouds of dust. Better cover your eyes."

They all did so. The man was right. There was such a crash and so much dust that nobody could see or hear what had really happened. When the dust cleared they all looked in the "chimney thing." And there it was! It was a large black leather bag lying on the ground behind the stone.

Everyone shouted.

"Don't touch it," said the workman. "I'll get Dr. Osgood."

The doctor could hardly believe what he saw. "I did miss it after all," he said. "And now let's see what's in the bag."

Everyone watched as Dr. Osgood worked carefully and slowly. Even so, the leather cracked under his gentle fingers. At last he got it open and pulled out an enormous teapot as black as coal.

"Solid silver," he said quietly.

"Silver?" cried Benny. "It looks more like iron."

"It's silver, just the same," said the doctor. "Wait until it is polished and you'll see—a real French piece that belonged to royalty."

Then he drew out a candlestick with six branches. It, too, was black. A large black pitcher came next, all covered with the same deep, fancy pattern that decorated the other pieces. Then Dr. Osgood pulled out a black box. A little black key hung on a black chain.

Dr. Osgood turned the key very gently. Inside was a necklace of gold, set with red and green stones.

"That's a queen's necklace," said Dr. Osgood. "That thing alone is a great treasure."

Under the necklace were gold coins of France. There was only one more thing in the bag. It was a roll of heavy paper.

"I may not be able to open this," said Dr. Osgood. "I shall stop if it begins to tear."

But he was so slow and gentle that the paper did not tear. He took one look. "It's in French," he said. "Of course it would be."

Both Henry and Jessie could read French. The old faded message was short.

"This is for my Indian friend Running Deer who saved my life. Louis Paul Deauville."

"That settles it!" said Benny. "This belongs to Lovan. And now who will tell Lovan?"

Nobody spoke for a minute. They all looked at each other.

Then Grandfather said with a smile, "David Walking-by-Night will tell Lovan."

CHAPTER 12

The Treasure

David looked puzzled when Mr. Alden chose him to tell Lovan.

"Mr. Alden, why me?" he asked.

Mr. Alden answered, "You know all about it, David, and you remember your grandmother. That will please Lovan. She is a fine person to have for a great-aunt."

Just then they heard the helicopter.

"Lunch!" cried Benny.

Henry looked at his watch. "Did you know it was two o'clock? How did you ever stand it, Ben?"

"I was so interested in that chimney thing," said Benny, "and the leather bag. I never thought of lunch."

"Now you know how *I* feel," said Dr. Osgood. "I forget all about eating."

Mr. Carter said, "Jessie, give me one sandwich. I'll go right back with the helicopter. I have some telephoning to do."

They all wondered what it was about. But nobody asked a question. They just said goodbye. And back went the helicopter down the mountain.

Mr. Carter carefully held the leather bag. Mr. Alden had given it to him.

After lunch, Dr. Osgood and his head man stayed on Flat Top. But the rest began to climb down. They were eager to tell Lovan what had happened.

"But let's not tell her the news too suddenly." Jessie said. "It might be too much all at once."

"Yes," agreed Henry. "Maybe it would be a good idea if she met David first and then heard about the treasure."

Violet said, "I think that is a good plan. Lovan can make up her mind about David and then he can tell her about the treasure."

When they reached Lovan's cottage, they found her sitting on the dinosaur step with a rough flat stone beside her. She was rubbing something on it.

Lovan had five white beads on a string. She had the string over her hand and was rubbing the white beads on the rough rock. The white pieces got rounder and rounder.

"You're making beads!" cried Benny.

"Yes. I have almost finished," said Lovan. "This is the last string." They saw two boxes of round beads, one of white and one of purple beads.

Lovan went on. She saw that they wanted to know. "I break a clamshell in small pieces," she said. "I make a small hole in every piece and string a few on a string. Then I grate them until they are round."

"I never knew that," said Mr. Alden. "I always wondered how wampum was made."

"This is how it is done," said Lovan. "Nobody uses

wampum now. But I sometimes weave it into my baskets."

All this time David had been watching Lovan. But Lovan was so busy she did not see David at all. Even Mr. Alden was a bit nervous now. He didn't quite know how Lovan would feel about meeting her nephew. But Lovan herself settled that. Suddenly she looked up at Mr. Alden and saw David behind him.

"An Indian boy!" she said. "Who are you, little brother?"

David said, "Well, I suppose I am your grandnephew and you are my Great-Aunt Lovan."

Lovan did not speak. She was thinking. She was looking David over. At last she said, "Then that baby did not die?"

"I guess not," said David, smiling a little. "I feel alive. My grandmother was named Susan. My mother died first, then Grandmother. I thought I was the last of my family."

Lovan nodded. She looked at David sharply. "A good young man, are you?"

David bowed his head. "I'm going to be. I can help you with your garden. Maybe I can go to school?"

Jessie and Henry were watching Lovan closely. They knew by the look on her face that Lovan was really very tired—tired of living alone, tired of walking so far to get sweet grass, and tired of wondering what would become of her.

Mr. Alden fixed it all up as well as he could. He said, "Lovan, you don't know David and he doesn't know you. But you can get to know each other. David can do work for the rangers at first and come to see you often. Then if you get along well, he can live here and take care of you. He's a strong young man."

Lovan put the beads in the box with the rest. "Come in," she said. "I will show you where David could sleep if he came here."

They all went into the cottage and Lovan opened a door.

David looked at the smooth bed. He looked at Lovan's kind face. For the first time in a long, long time David felt that he had a home and someone to care about him.

Before David could say anything there was a whistle. It came loud and clear into the little cottage.

"It's Mr. Carter!" said Jessie. "He always whistles that tune when he feels fine."

John Carter had a large box. He said, "I thought that Lovan ought to see her treasure."

"Oh, did you find the leather bag?" cried Lovan.

"Yes, we did," said Benny. "We came to tell you, but we wanted you to meet David first. Now don't be disappointed when you see the things. They look black but they're silver. They have to be polished."

"Of course," said Lovan. "The silver would turn black after all those years."

She looked at each piece. But the thing she seemed to like best was the paper with the French writing. Jessie told her what each French word meant.

"Poor man!" said Lovan. "He was shot by an Indian. When Great-Grandfather found him on the side of the mountain, he took care of him. He gave him all the good Indian medicines. But the poor man was badly hurt and knew it. He did not live long. I never heard where he was buried."

"It was secret, just like the bag," said Benny.

Mr. Alden packed the things in the box again. He gave the roll of paper to Lovan. He said, "Now if you agree, I'll sell these things to a museum or a collector and put the money in the bank. Nobody can get it out except you."

"And you, too, Mr. Alden," said Lovan. "I'd feel better if you could get it out, too. Something might happen to me."

"Very well. I'll fix it that way. And now you are tired. We'll go back to the motel. Come on, everybody."

Benny said, "It looks as if we've just about solved another mystery."

They all went out of the cottage and down the step. All but David. He stood on the step beside Lovan with his head down. He said to Lovan, "Do you mind if I bring my dog here? He's a good dog and he minds me."

"No," said Lovan, shaking her head. "I need a watchdog."

The two Indians looked at each other—one so old and one so young.

Lovan said a few soft words in an Indian language.

David answered her in the same language. They looked at each other and smiled. Then they shook hands.

David turned to Mr. Alden. "I'll come down later, sir. I'd like to stay here with Aunt Lovan for a little while, if you don't mind."

"No," said Mr. Alden, walking down to the station wagon, "I don't mind at all. It's exactly what I want most."

CHAPTER 13

No Goodbyes

When the family met at supper, David was not there.

"Don't worry about him," Mr. Alden said, sitting down at the table. "He's got two good legs and he can walk miles. He'll show up when he gets ready."

Mr. Carter was not there, either. Nobody asked where he was. They were used to his going and coming.

But Dr. Osgood was there. He said, "I shall be working here most of the summer. You know, my head man is a fine young scientist. He is having the time of his life. He knows those fossils even better than I do."

Benny had been looking thoughtful. Suddenly he said, "Why don't we go home, Grandfather?"

Everybody stopped eating to stare at Benny. He was usually the last person to want to go home.

"Well, why not?" Benny went on. "I'd like to see Watch again. We've been away quite a few days."

"That's an idea," said Grandfather. "Our real work here is ended. I shall keep track of David anyway, and Lovan, too. We can get here anytime in two hours."

Jessie said, "David will be a different boy, Grandfather. I think his Indian friends didn't treat him well. He was not from their tribe. If he's treated right, he'll act right."

Just as she spoke, a figure appeared in the door. It was David and he was indeed a changed boy. The whole family stared at him and listened.

"Oh, Mr. Alden!" he cried. (This didn't sound like David at all!) "My aunt and I are going to be fine together. She needs me, and I sure need a family." He put out both his hands to shake hands. "Aunt Lovan talks now, a steady stream!"

"So do you, Dave," said Benny, laughing. "What are you going to do first?"

"Well, I'm going to get my dog."

"What kind of a dog is he?" asked Jessie.

"Oh, he's a hound dog. He came to me. He didn't have any home either. He's white with black and sort of yellow. He has long soft ears. His tail wags so fast you can't see it."

Everyone was thinking the same thing, "David loves his dog."

"What's his name?" asked Violet.

David stopped short. Then he said, "I hate to tell you. I always called him *Mine*. He was the only thing I had."

"That's OK," said Benny. "When you call him, you can say Miney, Miney, Miney!"

"I never have to call him," said David, shaking his head. "He's always with me."

Grandfather said, "Sit down, my boy, and eat your supper. Don't you want a ride to Maine?"

"No. I'll go the same way I came. It won't take me long."

"We are going home, too, Dave," said Henry. "We want to get that silver cleaned and sold. And Grandfather wants to buy your aunt's woodland on both sides of Flat Top. When he owns it, Lovan can be sure the trees will not be cut. Mr. Carter knows collectors who buy old silver."

"And that necklace," said Jessie. "Lovan doesn't need to worry about money again."

"She's going to pay me by the week," said David. "I'll have to buy some heavy clothes if I work outdoors and some clothes for school, too."

"David!" said Grandfather. "I won't worry about you another minute. You are a man for sure. And that's what your Aunt Lovan needs—a strong young man. I know you must be disappointed that this treasure isn't yours, but—"

"Never mind that, Mr. Alden!" said David, putting

out his hand. "I don't want to hear it. Just wait till I get my dog. Then we'll be all set."

"We'll go to see your aunt later and say goodbye," said Grandfather, "and now we will say goodbye to you for awhile."

David pushed back his chair. His supper was finished. He looked at them all, one by one. He said, "But I don't know—I don't know—" Violet had tears in her eyes.

"Don't say anything, Dave," she said. "Just don't say anything."

Benny said, "I can't say goodbye to Dave, either."

"I know what you mean," Jessie said. "Dave is a good friend and it seems as if we have known him for a long time."

The next day was spent getting ready to leave. Mr. Alden wanted to talk with Dr. Osgood. He also wanted to see the rangers about Lovan Dixon and David.

Late in the afternoon the family drove over to see Lovan. They found her sitting on her dinosaur step, finishing a basket.

Somehow Lovan seemed different to them. There was a new happiness in her face.

"I have been looking for you," she said.

"You have?" asked Benny.

"Yes, the ranger told me," said Lovan. "He came over with my canned stuff. I have to get powdered milk for David. When you see him again you won't know him. I'm a good cook."

"He looks better already," said Grandfather. "David stands straight now and looks you right in the eye."

While Mr. Alden was telling Lovan about her woodlands and the treasure, the girls watched her fingers with the basket. They saw that she had put white beads all around the top of the basket. Now she was winding a border of sweet grass for the edge. She came to the last stitch and fastened the grass very tightly. She held it up a minute and then started to get up.

"Come in," she said.

She walked across the room and took another basket from the table. It was just like the other basket, but the beads were light purple. She turned around and gave the white one to Jessie and the purple one to Violet.

"A sewing basket for you," she said, "made with love."

The girls were so pleased that they could hardly speak.

"We need these so much!" said Jessie. She smelled the sweet grass.

"We'll always think of you when we use these," said Violet. "It is the nicest present you could have given us."

"Thank you, Lovan," said Grandfather. "Those are very thoughtful presents, and they are all your handiwork."

"Do sit down," said Lovan. She knew the young people would sit on the floor at her side.

"One more thing," said Grandfather, "if you are going to feed David and pay him by the week, you'll need money before I can buy this land. Now this is *my* business. I want David to be educated. And here is some money to start on. A ranger will come to bring you money. You make out a check and he will cash it. You'll be surprised how much a boy can eat."

"And a dog, too," said Lovan, smiling. She took the money. "I will take care of David like a son. I can teach him many things myself. And there is a school not too far away."

"Well," said Mr. Alden, getting up, "we must go. We'll just say goodbye for now."

"No, no!" cried Lovan. "Don't say goodbye. Say, 'Come again.' "

"That's the way to talk," said Benny. "We'll say come again soon, so why say goodbye?"

CHAPTER 14

Time for Celebration

The Aldens had been gone only one day when David came back from Maine with his dog.

It was night when David came, but he was sure of his way through the woods. He and his dog made almost no noise, but David found Lovan at the door of her cottage, waiting and listening.

The old Indian woman was smiling. She liked the way the dog trotted at David's side.

"This is Mine, Aunt Lovan," David said. "Let him sniff at you, then speak to him. He won't bite."

But Lovan knew what to do better than David. She opened the door wide so that the dog could smell the cooking. It was a delicious pot roast cooking with turnips and carrots and onions and potatoes. The dog trotted happily into the cottage. He turned to Lovan and sat up with his two front paws hanging down.

"He's smiling," cried David. "Doesn't that look like a smile?"

"Good dog," said Lovan. "Shake hands."

Now Mine had never learned to shake hands. But when the old lady took his paw in her hand he wagged his tail as well as he could while sitting on it. He seemed to know that Lovan was the one with the supper.

"Your supper is too hot, Miney," she said. "It's just right for you, David. Sit right down. Are you about starved?"

"Very near," said David. "I didn't want to stop to eat. But now it must be the middle of the night."

"It's one o'clock," said Lovan. She began to cut many thin slices off the meat. Then she piled a soup plate with vegetables. She put corn muffins on another plate and poured a large glass of milk. Mine sat still watching every move.

David said, "We ought not give Miney good meat like this. He eats scraps."

"Well, some other time, David," said Lovan. "Tonight it is a party."

"Miney is glad," said David. "I'll cut some of my meat for him. It's cool enough now. He likes everything—bread and vegetables and candy."

Mine wagged his tail all the time he was eating. He licked up the last bit and went over to Lovan and put both paws on her lap.

"Good dog," she said, patting his head. "You are mine, too."

"I'm glad you like him," said David.

"Did you have any trouble with the other Indians?" asked Lovan.

"No. They didn't want my dog. They have two or three others. I didn't even tell them where I was going. They didn't ask."

"I see," said Lovan. "And now let's all go to bed."

Things went along well and a month soon went by. Then the Aldens came back. As they drove into the woods they heard a dog barking.

"That's Miney!" said Benny, laughing.

Just then David and Lovan appeared around the corner of the house. The dog barked.

"Quiet," said David. He stopped.

The Aldens could hardly believe what they saw. "You must have gained ten pounds, Dave!" shouted Benny.

"I guess so," said David, laughing. He was delighted to see his good friends.

"What are you working on behind the house?" asked Henry.

"Come and see," said Lovan with a smile. "We are both outdoor people. So Dave made this place to eat."

Under the great pine trees was a large wooden table. On each side was a bench.

"The benches are long so we can have company," said David.

"Company like us!" shouted Benny.

"Let me show you what else we are doing, Mr. Alden," said David. "Aunt Lovan and I are making an Indian book."

"Let me see it. That is the best thing I have heard yet," said Mr. Alden. "We don't want to lose the best parts of Indian life."

By this time the Aldens were in the house, looking at the Indian book pages.

"It isn't half done yet," said David. "We are writing down the old stories in the Indian language. And we have drawn Indian pictures to go with them. We are trying to make them look like the ones Indians used to draw. Then Aunt Lovan is telling how to make designs. Here is a design for a basket, and here is one for a blanket. We both remember songs, but I have to learn how to write them down."

Just then Mr. Carter put his head in the door. He said to Lovan, "If you are worrying about feeding this crowd, we brought dinner for everyone."

"Thanks for telling me," said Lovan. "Really I haven't enough food for everyone. But we can cook whatever you have. Look over there. See what David built?"

It was an outdoor fireplace made of stones.

"Just in time!" yelled Benny. "Because we've got real steak today. We're celebrating!"

When they all sat down at last, Mine went under the

table and lay down on Henry's feet. Benny looked under the table. He said, "I do wish you'd choose my feet, Miney. But I suppose Henry makes you think of David. He's about the same size."

Everyone was talking. Violet was talking to David. Benny was talking to Lovan. Jessie was talking to Mr. Carter. Henry looked at Grandfather. "What a noise!" he said.

"But a good noise," said Grandfather. "Listen and you'll hear all the news."

Lovan was telling Benny that David had bought her a warm blanket with her new money. David was telling Violet that Lovan had made colors to paint with from things in the woods. Mr. Carter told Jessie that David was going to school in the fall.

"David is going to be even busier," said Grandfather. "Dr. Osgood tells me that he has tried him out on the mountain, and he's going to hire him as a helper in the summers."

"I didn't know there were such interesting things in the world," David said.

So here was David Walking-by-Night with a real job, and a new aunt, and a family to help him, and a good hound dog. What more could he want?

When the Aldens packed up to go, Benny said, "No we won't say it! We'll say we'll 'come again soon.' "

So that was it—come again—no goodbye.

On the way home, Benny said, "Oh, by the way, what will we do next summer, Grandfather?"

"Don't you wish you knew!" teased Grandfather.

"You mean *you* know?"

"I didn't say so, did I?"

"No, but your face looked so."

"Dear me," said Grandfather, "I must be more careful about my face!"

Benny teased for quite awhile. Then he stopped for he knew that Grandfather would not tell them until he got ready.

"Well, it's OK with me," he said at last. "Anyway whatever we do will be another story, huh, Gramps?"